The Shoemaker and the Elves

Retold and Illustrated by

I L S E   P L U M E

Harcourt Brace Jovanovich, Publishers

San Diego   New York   London

HBJ

Copyright © 1991 by Ilse Plume

Requests for permission to make copies of any part of
the work should be mailed to: Permissions Department,
Harcourt Brace Jovanovich, Publishers, Orlando, Florida 32887.

Library of Congress Cataloging-in-Publication Data
Plume, Ilse.
The shoemaker and the elves/retold and illustrated
by Ilse Plume from a tale by the Brothers Grimm. — 1st ed.
p.   cm.
Summary: A poor shoemaker becomes successful with
the help of four elves who finish his shoes during the night.
ISBN 0-15-274050-3
[1. Fairy tales.   2. Folklore — Germany.]   I. Wichtelmänner.
English. II. Title.
PZ8.P727   1991
398.2'1'0943 — dc19   88-26792

First edition   A B C D E

The illustrations in this book were done
in colored pencils on Strathmore drawing paper.
The display and text type were set in Centaur
by Thompson Type, San Diego, California.
Color separations were made by
Bright Arts, Ltd., Singapore.
Printed and bound by Tien Wah Press, Singapore
Production supervision by Warren Wallerstein
and Michele Green
Designed by Ilse Plume and Camilla Filancia

For Jane and Bill Langton
and
Mary and Lamar Soutter
— Ilse

Poor Antonio the shoemaker! When he was an old man in Italy, his luck went bad, and overnight he lost his fortunes to the wind.

"The larder is empty," said his wife, Bettina, who was a seamstress. "What shall we do?"

"I don't know," said Antonio. "There is nothing left on my workbench but the leather for one more pair of shoes."

Sadly he sat in his workshop, with his cat, Tomasina, on his lap. "There, there," he said, softly stroking her. "No fresh fish for you today, only leftover tails and fins."

That night Antonio cut out the leather so he would be ready to start working first thing in the morning. Then he locked the front door, blew out the candle, said his prayers, and went to bed.

As soon as the rooster crowed in the morning, Antonio jumped out of bed, eager to begin work. To his great astonishment, a miracle awaited him in his workshop — a brand-new pair of shoes, all finished and beautifully made. He couldn't believe his eyes! The shoes were perfect, down to the very last stitch.

Before Antonio had time to run and tell Bettina what had happened, a customer came and bought the shoes. They were just the right size. She was so pleased with them she paid double. There was money for Antonio to buy enough leather for two more pairs of shoes and some fresh fish for Tomasina.

That evening the shoemaker prepared the leather. He was so happy he whistled as he cut the pattern for two pairs of fine boots. Bettina sang while she made the supper, and Tomasina purred contentedly. When at last the clock struck ten, Antonio tumbled into bed, pleased with his day's work.

Once again as the rooster's crow announced the beginning of a new day, Antonio bounded out of bed. To his surprise there were two new pairs of boots on the workbench, as beautifully made as the shoes of the night before. Again customers came and paid very good prices for them.

This time the shoemaker had enough money to buy leather for four pairs of shoes. And so it continued, until at last he was prosperous again.

But who was making all the beautiful shoes? At first Antonio did not want to question his good fortune. Then, one evening just before Christmas, he said, "Bettina, why don't we stay up tonight and see who does this magic?"

Bettina agreed wholeheartedly. They lit a candle and left it on the table in the workshop. Then they hid behind a curtain in the pantry.

Just as the cuckoo clock chirped midnight, four elves slipped in through a broken shutter and sat down on the workbench. Antonio and Bettina watched in amazement as the elves began to hammer and stitch. All night long the elves worked busily, with never a yawn. When the first rays of sunlight came through the shutters, they ran away through the garden. The elves were so quiet, the sound of their little feet scurrying over the tiles didn't even wake Tomasina.

At breakfast Bettina said, "Antonio, we really must find a way to show our thanks to these little elves. They have saved us from our misfortune. I have some fine cloth left in my sewing basket. It should be just enough for some new clothes for the elves. For new jackets and pants, and even some shirts and vests. I'll knit them each a pair of striped stockings, and you can make them some lovely little boots."

"A wonderful plan!" said Antonio, and they set to work.

The next day was Christmas Eve. Instead of leaving the leather on the table as usual, they piled up their gifts, wrapped in brightly colored paper and ribbons. Then they lit the candle and hid in the pantry once more.

At midnight the elves crept into the house, eager to begin working. But instead of leather and scissors and hammers, they found brightly wrapped presents! At first they were puzzled, but their surprise turned to joy when they opened the presents and discovered the lovely clothes and boots. Quickly they changed into their new finery and danced around in delight, singing:

> Look at us! We're fine to see,
> No longer cobblers must we be.

Hopping and skipping, they jumped over all the tables and chairs, until at last they danced out the door.

From that time to this, the elves have never been seen again.
Once more Antonio makes the shoes and boots himself. But all
the people of the town come to his workshop to buy them. If
you stop by his shop some morning, you are sure to find him in.
Bettina will be working in her garden. And take care not to step
on Tomasina, stretched out in the sun beneath your feet!